This

A little Courage

Taltal Levi

North
South

Every morning I rise with the sun.

During the day I play
and have fun.

I search the house for little treasures.
Sometimes I stumble on the most curious things.

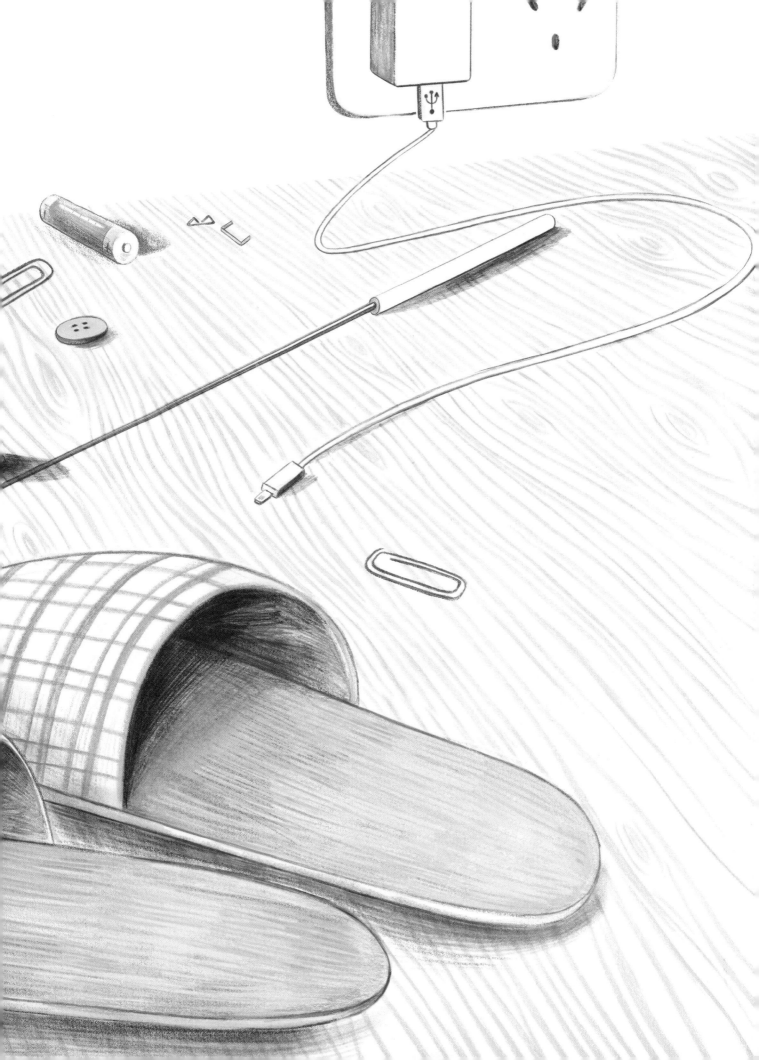

I help myself to a glass of water on the warmer days.

And I go on quests and adventures
among the leaves and stems.

But today is unlike any other as I am being followed by a dark, scary shadow.

Must I hide now forever?

No! This is my house and I will not hide!
And with a little courage...

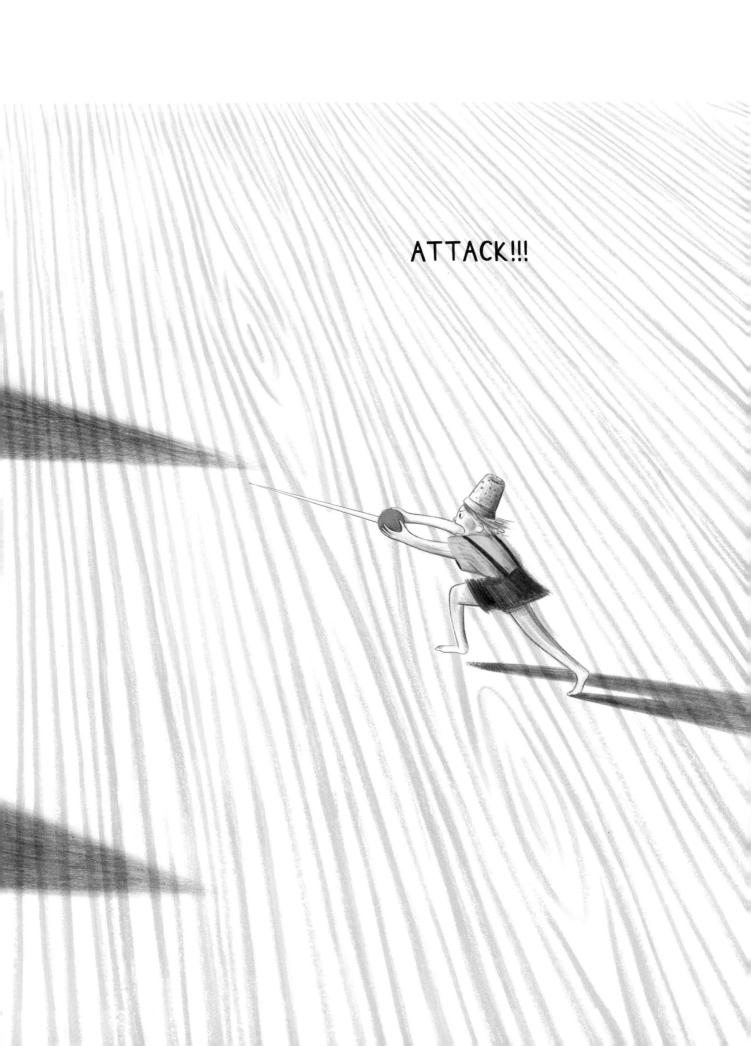

What are you!?

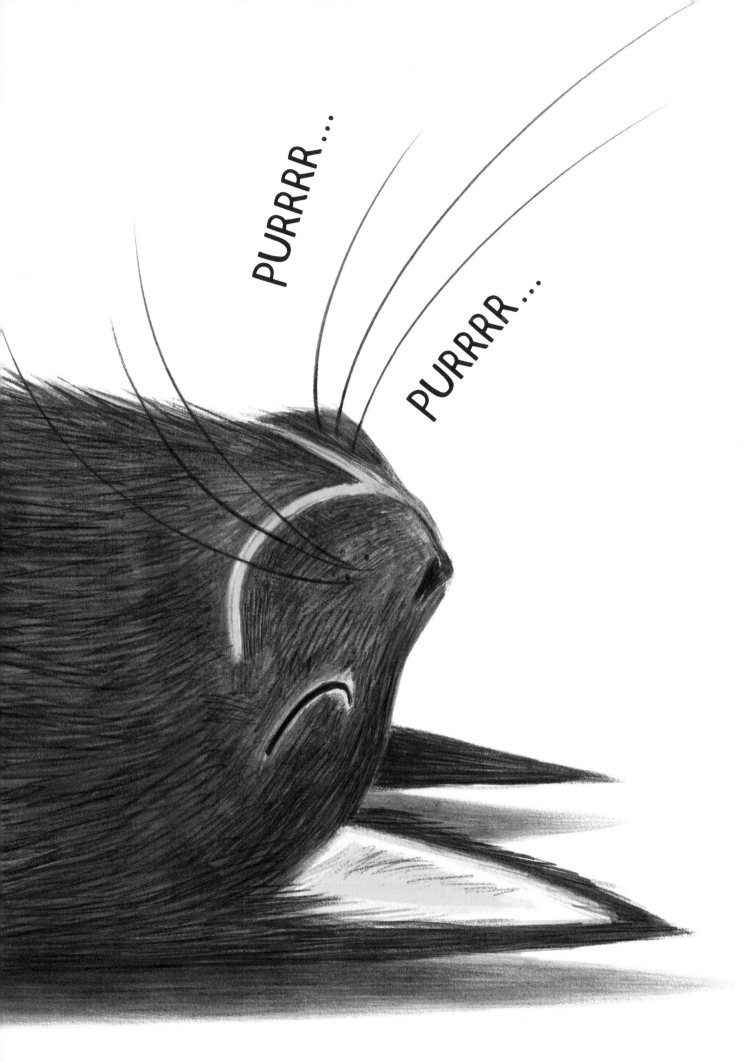

Easy now. ...
Can I really trust you?

Dear scary shadow,
you seem so gentle and nice.

Let us be friends and explore the house.

From this day on we rise
together with the sun.

During the day we play
and have fun.

We search the house for treasures.
Sometimes we stumble on the most
delicious things.

We help ourselves to a cool bath
when the days get warm.

And we go on quests and adventures beyond
the front door. . . .

And who are you?

To my family—T.L.

Text and pictures: Taltal Levi
Mentor: Evelyne Laube

Text and illustrations copyright © 2018 by Taltal Levi.
First published in Switzerland under the title *Ein Fingerhut voll Mut*.
English text copyright © 2020 by NorthSouth Books, Inc., New York 10016.

First published in the United States, Great Britain, Canada, Australia, and New Zealand in 2020
by NorthSouth Books, Inc., an imprint of NordSüd Verlag AG, CH-8050 Zürich, Switzerland.

Distributed in the United States by NorthSouth Books, Inc., New York 10016.
Library of Congress Cataloging-in-Publication Data is available.
ISBN: 978-0-7358-4394-3

1 3 5 7 9 · 10 8 6 4 2
Printed in Latvia 2019
www.northsouth.com

Taltal Levi was born in the Galilee, Israel. She graduated from Lucerne University of Arts and Design with a degree in illustration, and currently works and lives in Basel, Switzerland.

From a young age she used drawing as a tool to liberate herself from reality's hardship and dullness. Taltal loves telling stories about characters who embrace their vulnerabilities and overcome obstacles. Her narratives incorporate fantasy elements and draw inspiration from nature, animals and her own childhood memories.
For more information visit: www.taltallevi.com

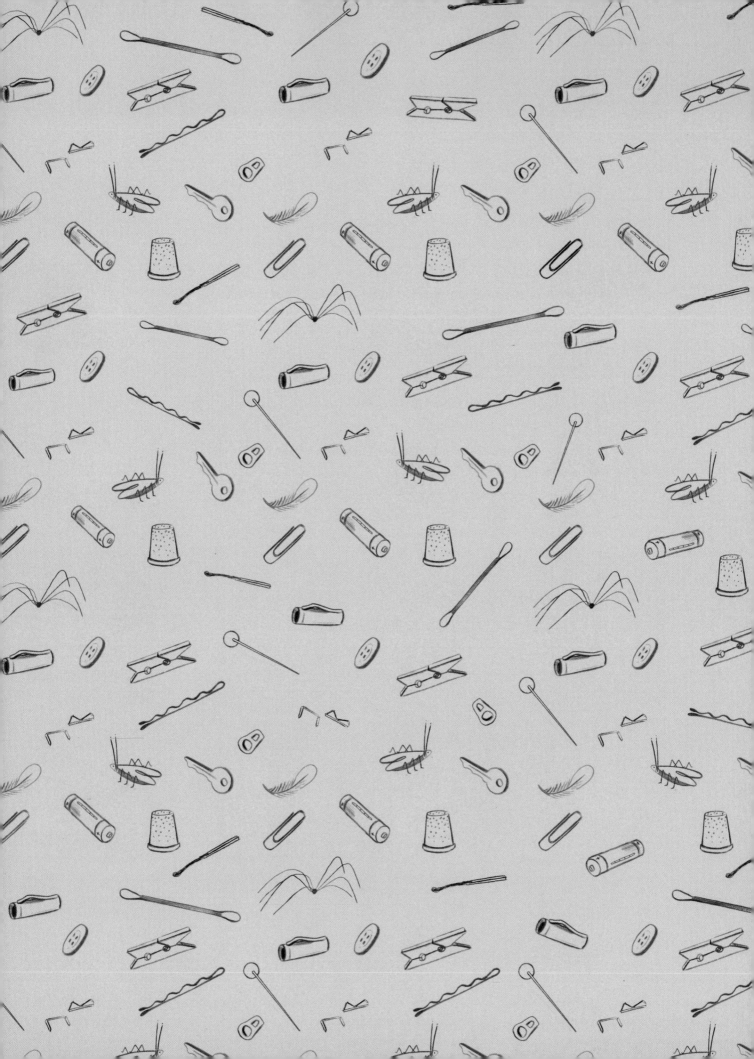